The Christmas Mouse

Stephanie Jeffs and Jenny Thorne

It was snowing hard.
The black cat was prowling in the backyard.
The little mouse hid in the roots of the thick hedge,
watching the large flakes of snow fall gently to the ground.

Slowly he moved from his hiding place,
looking carefully around him.
There was no cat to be seen.

*S*uddenly, the cat pounced, almost catching the tail of the little mouse with her claws.

The mouse darted up the yard, leaping up the stony bank toward the big house, too frightened to look back.

Then he saw it—the perfect place.

The little mouse scurried inside. He crept along as far as he could and then lay still, darkness all around him.

He lay in the toe of the big boot and waited.

He thought of the cat looking for him, tail slowly moving, whiskers twitching.

Then the mouse heard
a voice.

"Sooty!" the voice
called. "Come here, Sooty!
You're soaking wet!"

The little mouse heard
the black cat purring.

"No, you don't!" said
the voice firmly. "I'm not
having your wet paws in the
house tonight! You can sleep
in the shed."

The cat meowed sulkily.
But the mouse heard the door
close firmly and the footsteps
disappear.

"Matthew!" called the
voice again. "You'd better
bring your boots in. It's
snowing hard outside."

The little mouse scrambled to the toe of the boot as it swung high in the air. Then the boot fell and toppled over.

The house was warm. The mouse could hear the slow tick-tock, tick-tock, of a clock.

The mouse crept out of the boot. The carpet was warm under his feet.

He made his way along the baseboard in the dark. Then he pushed through a small crack . . .

. . . and found himself in the most beautiful place he had ever seen!

The dying embers of the fire cast an orange glow around the room, and in the corner was a wonderful tree. The little mouse had seen many trees before, but never one quite like this. Its branches were covered with delicate silver strands hanging like icicles. And at the foot of the tree lay many shapes, all covered in pictures, ribbons, and bows.

The mouse moved closer and stared. At the very top of the tree there was a beautiful figure, dressed in white. Lower down the mouse saw a star and some candles.

At the bottom of the tree, something caught his eye. It was a picture of a mouse.

13

He climbed onto the package and carefully sniffed the paper.

Suddenly the present slid off the top of the pile, and the little mouse fell with it, clawing the paper to keep his balance.

Mouse and present landed heavily on the floor.

The mouse's claws had made large holes in the paper. He put his head inside the present and burrowed around.

He ripped back the paper, nibbled through the ribbon, and stood on the cover of a book. He pushed his nose under the cover; then, easing his body forward, the little mouse slid under it.

Down, down, down, the little mouse suddenly found himself falling— twisting and turning, head over tail, until . . . he landed and lay still, eyes closed, body shaking.

His nose twitched as he smelled the familiar smell of cows and sheep, straw and hay.

The straw made his nose tickle, and he sneezed.

"Shh!" said a voice behind him.

The little mouse jumped.

"Shh!" said the voice again.

He opened his eyes and saw behind him a small grey mouse.

The grey mouse pointed to the figures of two human beings huddled together.

"Waaahhh!" A small cry went up, and the figures moved.

The two mice watched as the man gently put his arm around the woman.

"Isn't he beautiful, Joseph?" the woman asked, rocking the baby in her arms.

The man smiled and nodded.

"Yes, Mary," he said. "He's beautiful."

The grey mouse turned to the little mouse.

"You're not from Bethlehem, are you?" he asked. "A visitor, I suppose? You'd better come with me."

"You've come on a very special night," said the grey mouse. "God promised that it would be, and it's not over yet."

"Who?" asked the little mouse.

"Why, God, of course!" said the grey mouse. "God, who made everything: the world, the stars, the planets, the trees, the people, the cows, the dogs, the sheep, the cats . . ."

"Cats?"

"Yes, cats—and mice," added the grey mouse. "He made

everything. But you must be hungry. Have something to eat."

The little mouse sank onto the floor of the mouse hole and ate. And as he ate, he told the story of how he came to be there: the cat, the boot, the beautiful room, and finally, the book. The grey mouse listened, his eyes growing bigger and wider.

"What a story!" he said.

"Yes," said the little mouse. "I won't blame you if you don't  believe me. It's all so incredible."

"Oh, I believe you," said the grey mouse. "After all, incredible things sometimes happen."

"Do they?" replied the little mouse, surprised.

"Well," said the grey mouse, "what's happened here tonight is even more incredible. That baby born tonight—well, it's a very special baby. It is God's only Son, Jesus. God has given him to the world as a gift, a present!"

*T*he grey mouse paused.

"Listen!"

They strained to hear muffled sounds. Then the grey mouse took the little mouse firmly by the neck and pulled him out of the hole.

All around them were stamping hooves, while the air was filled with the sound of bleating sheep.

"Up here!" shouted the grey mouse, and he pushed the little mouse to the top of a large bale of hay.

The mice sat and watched the shepherds below them, who were panting as if they had hurried there, while everywhere there was the noise of bleating animals.

The woman called Mary moved toward the manger, which she had made into a cradle. She bent down to pick up the baby.

Then there was a hushed silence.

One by one, the shepherds sank to their knees.

"The angel was right," whispered one shepherd to another. "This baby is the Savior of the world."

He turned to Mary and Joseph.

"We saw an angel, out in the fields," he explained. "He said if we came to Bethlehem, we would find a baby in a manger."

"At first we were terrified!" said another. "One moment it was pitch dark; the next, the sky was filled with light, and there was a voice telling us not to be afraid."

"When I heard the voice," continued the first shepherd, "I looked up and saw an angel, a messenger from God, and I wasn't frightened anymore."

Then in a jumble of excited words, the shepherds told their story of how from nowhere, the sky was full of angels, all praising God, filling the night air with beautiful sounds.

"What did the angels sing?" asked Mary.

"They sang, 'Glory to God in the highest, and peace to his people on earth,' " said the shepherds.

"Glory to God in the highest," repeated Mary and Joseph, "and peace to his people on earth!"

"Glory to God in the highest . . ." said the grey mouse.

". . . and peace to his people on earth!" answered the little mouse. The words filled him with warmth and happiness.

"Glory to God!" he squeaked again from the hay bale.

The little mouse looked down at the little baby. At that moment he felt as if there was no one else in the world but himself and the baby lying in the manger: Jesus, God's Son.

Then there were
sounds again.

The shepherds stood up
and left the stable. As each one
left, he looked at the little baby
as if he was sorry to leave him.

Soon there was no one left
but Mary, Joseph, and the
baby, and the little mice
watching from the top of the hay
bale.

The dawn light gently
glowed under the door.

"Wasn't that wonderful?"
whispered the grey mouse.

The little mouse nodded.

26

"Now I understand," he said. "This baby really is very, very special. Jesus can be God's present to everyone."

The mice climbed down to the manger and peeped at the baby lying in the hay.

"We'd better go," said the grey mouse. "Over there . . . do you see that small hole in the corner?"

The little mouse nodded and scurried toward the hole. He squeezed through, pushing as hard as he could . . .

But instead of being outside, the little mouse felt himself being squeezed and pulled and tugged as he struggled and wriggled. He pushed until suddenly . . . he was free.

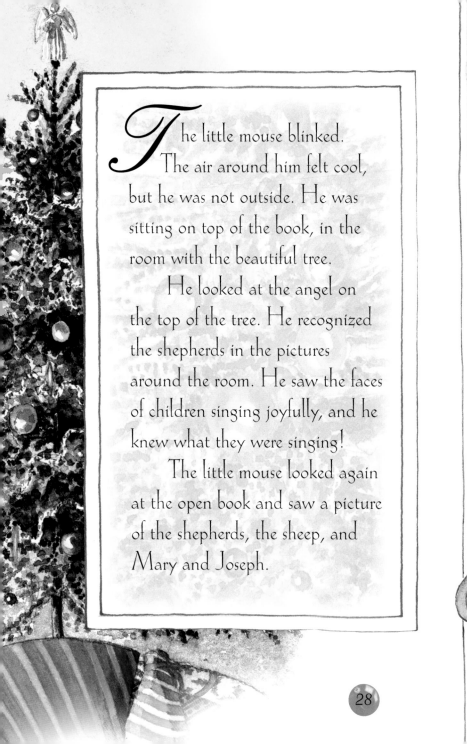

The little mouse blinked. The air around him felt cool, but he was not outside. He was sitting on top of the book, in the room with the beautiful tree.

He looked at the angel on the top of the tree. He recognized the shepherds in the pictures around the room. He saw the faces of children singing joyfully, and he knew what they were singing!

The little mouse looked again at the open book and saw a picture of the shepherds, the sheep, and Mary and Joseph.

And under the manger were two small mice. But he wasn't looking at the mice. He had his eyes fixed on the baby lying in the manger.

The little mouse stared at the picture for a while. Then somewhere, from the innermost part of his body, came the words he had repeated that night.

"Glory to God in the highest," he squeaked, "and peace to his people on earth!"

Very slowly the little mouse left the book. He moved toward the door and, taking one last look at the picture of the baby, left the room. He crawled into the boot . . . and waited to be set free in the backyard.

Published in the U.S. and Canada by
The Word Among Us Press
7115 Guilford Drive
Frederick Maryland 21704
www.wau.org

ISBN: 978-1-59325-194-9

First edtion 2005
Seventh printing 2017

Printed and bound in Malaysia
September 2017